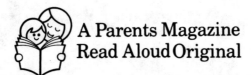

A Parents Magazine
Read Aloud Original

ONE LITTLE MONKEY

by **Stephanie Calmenson**
pictures by **Ellen Appleby**

Parents Magazine Press
New York

Text Copyright © 1982 by Stephanie Calmenson.
Illustrations Copyright © 1982 by Ellen Appleby.
All rights reserved.
Printed in the United States of America.
10 9 8 7 6 5

Library of Congress Cataloging in Publication Data.
Calmenson, Stephanie. One little monkey.
SUMMARY: Swinging through the trees in the jungle
because he's been stung by a bee, one monkey is
followed by groups of animals from two to ten who
think hunters must be pursuing them.
[1. Animals—Fiction. 2. Jungles—Fiction.
3. Counting. 4. Stories in rhyme.] I. Appleby,
Ellen, ill. II. Title.
PZ8.3.C130n 1982 [E] 82-7958
ISBN 0-8193-1091-3   AACR2
ISBN 0-8193-1092-1 (lib. bdg.)

For Mom and Dad
and Michael—S.C.

To my mother,
for all her help—E.A.

One little monkey
Sitting in a tree
Got stung on the tail
By a buzzing bumble bee.

The monkey started swinging
As fast as he could go.
Two hippos saw him racing by
And shouted from below,

"Is there trouble in the jungle?"
"Yes there is, indeed!"

So the hippos started running
At breakneck speed.

Now just behind the hippos
Three zebras stood out grazing.
And when they saw those hippos run
They thought it was amazing.

"It sure must be important,"
Said Zebra Number Three.
"I guess we'd better follow them.
Stay very close to me!"

The zebras started running
As quickly as they could
And passed four lively antelope
Playing in the wood.

"The hunters must be coming!
We can't waste any time."
And so they followed after
The quickly growing line.

There were monkey, hippos, zebras,
Antelope, and then
They ran into five lions
Roaring in their den.

"It has to be the hunters!"
Said the smallest one.
So they stopped what they were doing
And broke into a run.

"A game of tag?" said Big Baboon.
"Will you let us play?"
"No, no! It's hunters," Lion said.
And six baboons were on their way.

A herd of sleepy elephants
Cried, "Danger must be near!"

So seven husky elephants
Followed to the rear.

Eight parrots singing in a tree
Saw the herd pass by.
"It must be time to leave the nest!"
Then they began to fly.

Nine giraffes were eating lunch,
a meal of tasty leaves.

They heard the call to come along
And they caught up with ease.

Ten tigers playing leapfrog
Quickly took the hint.
"We *thought* we smelled some hunters."
And they began to sprint.

They had not traveled very far...

When everyone stopped short.
"Oh, no!" cried all the animals.
"Did someone just get caught?"

"Why are you stopping, monkey?
The hunters must be near.
And they are sure to catch us
If we are standing here!"

The monkey started laughing.
"There are no hunters — see?
I only had my tail stung
By a buzzing bumble bee."

But while the monkey laughed at them
The others turned and then —
Uh-oh, Little Monkey...

You just got stung again!

About the Author

Stephanie Calmenson says she wanted to write a story about Little Monkey as soon as she saw the monkey that Ellen Appleby had drawn in her sketchbook. "It's fun making up stories that way," she says.

In fact, the author hopes that the children who read this book might pick one of the animals in it and make up a story of their own.

Stephanie Calmenson has written and edited many books for children. She lives in New York City.